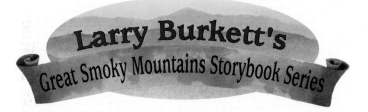

A Home for the Hamsters

Written by
Larry Burkett
with K. Christie Bowler

Illustrated by **Terry Julien**

MOODY PRESS
CHICAGO

Dedicated to
Morgan, Brianna, Matthew,
David, JonMarc, and Levi Burkett

Text & Illustrations ©1999 BURKETT & KIDS, LLC

Larry Burkett's Money Matters for Kids™
Executive Producer: *Allen Burkett*

For Lightwave
Managing Editor: *Elaine Osborne*
Art Director: *Terry Van Roon*
Desktop: *Andrew Jaster*

ISBN: 0-8024-0982-2
1 3 5 9 7 10 8 6 4 2
Printed in the United States of America

The Great Smoky Mountain Tales come to you from Larry Burkett's Money Matters for Kids™. In each tale, our family's children have fun while they learn how to best manage their money according to God's principles of stewardship.

This series of children's stories tells the adventures of the Carmichael family who live in a state park in the Great Smoky Mountains of North Carolina. The park is a beautiful setting, with a mist rising from the mountains like a smoky mist, giving them their name. Mom and Dad work in the park and, with their children Sarah, Joshua, and Carey, live in the rangers' compound not far inside the main park gate. Sarah, ten years old, is conscientious and loves doing things the right way. She has lots of energy, is artistic, and thinks before she acts. Her brother Joshua is eight and a half. Always doing something active, he's impulsive, adventurous, and eager to learn. Carey, their younger sister, is almost three and very cute. She loves doing whatever her sister and brother are doing. In the first four books of the series they learn how to save, how to give to the church, how to spend wisely, and how to earn money.

There's always something interesting going on in the Great Smoky Mountains, from hiking and horseback riding to fishing or panning for sapphires and rubies. Nearby, the town of Waynesville and, only a little farther away, the city of Asheville, provide all the family needs in the way of city amenities.

Through everyday adventures—from buying pet hamsters to dealing with the aftermath of a winter storm, from getting the right equipment in order to become an artist to going on summer camping trips—the children learn. Practical situations any child could face serve as the background for teaching about God's principles of stewardship.

Your children will love the stories and ask for more. Without even realizing it, they will, like our characters, learn in the middle of an adventure.

Sarah and Joshua pressed their noses against the Pet Store window in Waynesville. Two hamsters played in a cage just inside. The brown one with a white eye patch ran in place. His little black eyes twinkled as his exercise wheel spun around and around. The orange and white one burrowed through the shavings on the floor of the cage.

"They're so cute!" Sarah breathed dreamily.

"I'd like a hamster all my own," Joshua stated.

"Me, too."

Half buried, the orange and white hamster plowed through the shavings and surfaced right beside his food dish. His nose and whiskers twitched as he looked it over. Satisfied, he sat down right in the middle of it.

Joshua laughed. "Do you think Mom and Dad would let us have one?" he asked.

"Maybe," Sarah said. "Let's go ask!" She slung her backpack over her shoulder. "Race you to the car!" she yelled as she ran off. Joshua dashed after her.

As Mom drove home, Sarah said, "We saw the cutest hamsters in the Pet Store! Can we have one of our own?"

"Yes. Get hamsters!" their little sister Carey added.

"Let's all talk about it when we get home," Mom said as she drove through the entrance to the state park. She turned left off the main road through a gap in the trees toward their house.

In his Park Ranger's uniform, Dad was just climbing out of the Jeep. As soon as they pulled into the driveway, Joshua jumped out, calling, "Hey, Dad! We'd like some hamsters!

They're so cute and they don't take up much room and they would be good for us."

"Hmm." Dad thought, rubbing his chin. "Pets are a lot of work . . ."

"We can take care of hamsters," Sarah stated. Joshua nodded hard.

"We'll think about it," Dad said. Later, after talking with Mom, he told them, "You can get hamsters if you promise to look after . . ."

"We promise!" the kids said together.

Mom smiled. "You'll have to save up your money."

Joshua sighed. "How will I ever get enough money?"

"All you need is a plan," Dad said, getting envelopes and pens. "We'll show you."

Mom agreed. "When you get your allowance or money for extra jobs, divide it into . . . four envelopes. The first is for the church. Put 10 percent—ten cents of every dollar—in the church envelope." She wrote "Church" on two envelopes, one each for Sarah and Joshua.

"'Big Goal Savings,'" Dad said, labeling two envelopes, "is for big things—like a bicycle or college—that take months or years to save for. It gets twenty-five cents of every dollar."

Mom thought, then, writing on an envelope, continued, "'Small Goal Savings' is for things that take a few weeks to save for—like your hamster. It gets 25 percent too."

"What's the last one?" Joshua asked.

"Spending!" Mom smiled. "It gets the rest: forty cents of every dollar. You can spend it any way you want. You're good at that!" The kids laughed. "Whenever you get money, divide it into your envelopes. Soon you'll have enough for your hamsters!"

"And cages and starter kits," Dad added.

Sarah and Joshua wanted to buy their hamsters as soon as possible, so Mom and Dad found extra jobs for them.

On Saturday the sun shone out of a cloudless blue sky. As Sarah raked the colorful fall leaves into three big piles, she thought the Great Smoky Mountains State Park where her parents were Rangers was the perfect place to live!

Joshua filled a bucket and carried it to the kitchen window. He slopped water over the glass and started washing. After finishing his first set of windows, he grinned, jumped down from the box he was using and took a running leap right into the middle of Sarah's biggest pile of leaves!

"Hey!" Sarah yelled. Then she laughed and jumped in herself. Soon red and yellow leaves were stuck all over their clothes and hair. After playing, they went back to raking and washing. When they finished, they put their tools away and called Mom and Dad to inspect their work.

"Good job!" Dad said. When he paid them, Joshua and Sarah ran upstairs and happily divided the money into their envelopes.

That afternoon, Sarah and Joshua biked to the General Store near the main entrance to the park. They leaned their bikes against the wall and ran up the steps, the money from their Spending envelopes jingling in their pockets. They peered at the displays of candies, chocolate bars, jelly beans, and other goodies.

Sarah chose jelly beans and a couple of chocolate candies.

Joshua picked a small chocolate bar then wandered over to the toy section. His eyes gleamed as he looked at the

miniature cars. Finally, he chose a bright blue racing car and took it to the counter with his chocolate bar.

"How come you have enough money for a car, Josh?" Sarah asked.

"Oh, I took some out of my Small Goal Savings envelope," he answered. "I have lots of time to get more money for the hamster and cage, and I really want this car!"

"But . . . ," Sarah began, then she shrugged. Her Small Goal Savings money was staying in the envelope until she could buy her pet.

That week the kids did a couple of other little jobs to earn money. Then, on Friday just before supper, Mom called, "Allowance time!"

The quiet house burst into noise and activity. Sarah clattered down the stairs, Joshua raced in from the family room, and Carey joined them with a big smile.

Mom counted out each child's allowance in change so they could easily divide it into their envelopes. Sarah and Joshua took theirs and ran up to their rooms right away. They spread their envelopes on their beds and carefully divided their money into each envelope as they'd been taught: ten cents per dollar in the Church envelope; twenty-five cents per dollar each in Small Goal and Big Goal Savings; and forty cents per dollar for the Spending envelope.

Sarah had written, "Hamster, cage, and starter kit — $27.00" on her Small Goal Savings envelope. She counted the money in it. She could almost see the cute little hamster in his bright new cage right now! Grinning, she took fifty cents from her Spending envelope and added it to her Small Goal Savings.

The next afternoon Joshua and his friend Lee, another Ranger's son, wandered down to the General Store to look around. "Look at that!" Joshua breathed suddenly. "A Camper's All-in-One Kit. It has a magnifying glass, compass, spoon, fork, knife . . ."

"Tweezers . . . and look!" Lee pointed. "A fishhook and line!"

"I just gotta have this thing!" Joshua looked at the price. "Hey! I've got more than enough in my savings."

"I thought that was for a hamster and stuff," Lee said.

"Yeah, but this is cooler. I can get the hamster later.

These'll be sold in no time and it'll be too late." Joshua raced home on his bike and grabbed some money out of his Small Goal Savings envelope.

Dad called to him, "Hey, Josh, here's a job for you. It'll pay well."

"Can I do it later?" Joshua asked over his shoulder as he headed back to the General Store.

"I'll do it, Dad," Sarah offered eagerly. "I've just finished the job Mom gave me."

Dad smiled. "OK, Sarah. It should really be done this afternoon. It's yours."

A couple of days later, Joshua wandered into the family room with his All-in-One Kit. It wasn't as well made as he'd thought, but it was still cool. He watched Sarah fuss with a colorful cloth. "What's that?" he asked.

"It's a cover I made for my hamster's cage to help him sleep," Sarah answered. "And look! I've found him a little food dish." She proudly showed Joshua the lid that was just the right size. She'd also decorated an empty toilet roll for her hamster to play in. A "hamster care" book from the school library lay open on the floor. "I almost have enough money," she said. "I can hardly wait! Oh, I called the Pet Store," she added. "They said they only have the hamsters until next weekend. Then they'll have to send them back to their other store. How are you doing?"

Joshua's heart sank. Seeing Sarah's preparations and hearing her excitement made him realize he really did want a hamster. He looked at his Camper's All-in-One Kit and sighed. "I spent my money," he said sadly. "I don't have anywhere near enough now."

"What's wrong, Joshua?" Mom asked that night at supper.

"I want a hamster and cage but I spent my money on my camper's kit," Joshua said.

"Sounds like you changed your savings goal without really thinking about it," Dad commented. Joshua nodded, pushing his peas around his plate. "It's important to stick to your goal," Dad added. "Or to think it through and then change it. Ask yourself what you want most."

Joshua sighed, "A hamster."

"The difference between the Spending and the Savings

money," Mom explained, "is time. Savings is for things you don't have enough for right away. You have to decide if you want that thing enough to wait for it."

"I have an idea," Sarah said slowly. "What if our hamsters share a cage for a while?"

"Really?" Joshua's eyes lit up.

"You buy your hamster and his food. I'll buy the cage. To be fair, you can clean the cage more. Then, when you have enough, you can buy your own cage."

"All right!" Joshua shouted. "Thanks, Sarah."

That week Mrs. Scott, the owner of the General Store, heard that Joshua wanted to earn some money. On Saturday she hired him to pick up the trash and leaves from around the store and in her huge parking lot. Joshua had already done a couple of small jobs for Mom at home during the week. Now he took his garbage bags and broom and set to work. If he did a good job here, he should have just enough money to buy his hamster and food. He could hardly wait!

As Joshua worked, his friends Lee and Tony rode up on their bikes with their fishing poles. "Want to come fishing?" Lee asked.

It was a perfect day for fishing in the river. Joshua almost said yes, but he had to finish the job he'd agreed to do. And then he thought about his hamster. "Not today, Lee. I gotta finish cleaning the parking lot."

Lee and Tony waved and rode off. Joshua watched them go and then went back to work. He knew he'd made the right decision even if it took him the whole day to finish. He would have the money in time, he just knew it!

After Mrs. Scott inspected Joshua's work, she led him into the store and paid him. "You did a great job, Joshua."

He grinned and thought about buying a popsicle. Then he shook his head. The money was going into his Savings envelope! Mrs. Scott noticed Joshua eyeing the popsicles. "Go ahead and take one," she said. "A good job deserves a bonus."

"Thanks, Mrs. Scott!" Joshua chose an orange one and rode home with his money. He went right to his room to

divide his pay into his four envelopes. Then he carefully
counted out the money in his Small Goal Savings envelope.
He counted it twice. He couldn't believe it. He had enough!

"Hey, Sarah!" he called. "I've got it!" He ran into her
room and showed her.

"Way to go!" Sarah said. She got out her Small Goal
Savings envelope and counted out her money too. "And I
have enough for the cage, starter kit, and hamster!"

They grinned at each other and shouted, "Yes!"

Monday after school, the family piled into their car and headed into Waynesville to the Pet Store. Joshua and Sarah were so excited the only thing keeping them in their seats was their seatbelts. Carey wasn't sure what a hamster was, but she was excited too.

At the store, the kids looked over the hamsters carefully, searching for the happiest, cutest, and friendliest. Finally, they chose the ones they'd seen in the window earlier. Joshua took the brown one with the white eye patch and called him Pirate. Sarah called her orange and white one Huey. Then they chose their starter kit and bought food.

Joshua and Sarah took their purchases to the cashier and pulled out their Small Goal Savings envelopes. They counted out their money proudly and paid the cashier. They even had some left over!

When they had everything, they loaded their treasures in the car for the trip home. Pirate and Huey stuck their noses through the bars of their new cage to watch everything with bright, curious eyes.

That evening in Sarah's room the two children looked through the cage at their new friends. Pirate ran in place on the exercise wheel, making it spin around and around. His black eyes sparkled and his whiskers twitched as he concentrated. Huey was inside Sarah's colorful toilet roll. His nose and whiskers poked out of one end and his tail poked out of the other.

Sarah reached in and picked up Huey, toilet roll and all. When she put the roll on her lap, Huey crawled out and began exploring, tickling her with his tiny feet. Sarah giggled as he wandered over her legs and onto the carpet.

Joshua and Sarah grinned at each other.

"It was worth waiting for, wasn't it?" Sarah asked.

"Yup," Joshua agreed. "But next time I'll stick to my goal better." He picked up Pirate and held him so he could look him in the eye. "You are great!" he declared. "And just wait. Soon you'll have a cage all your own!"

Be an Ant

"You people who don't want to work, think about the ant! Consider its ways and be wise! . . . it stores up its food in summer. It gathers its food at harvest time" (Proverbs 6:6–8 NIrV).

You can probably come up with a list of things you'd like to have: that new toy or video game, a cool shirt, a meal at your favorite restaurant. How about a pair of roller blades? Or a new pet? Can you really save money and buy the things you'd like? Absolutely! All you have to do is be like an ant and start saving. It's as easy as 1–2–3–4–5:

1. Make a plan for your money, a budget, that matches your income, age, and needs. (See page 8–9 for one that will work for children up to age 12.)
2. Decide what you want and figure out how much it will cost. That's your savings goal.
3. Every time you get money, put the amount or percentage your plan says into your savings bank or envelope. Keep track of how much you have on a special piece of paper or in a savings journal.
4. When you reach your goal, go out and have fun buying what you saved for!
5. From then on, the money that used to go toward that goal goes toward your next goal.

Money with a Purpose

Saving a planned amount of money each month or week for a special goal gives great results. It helps you get enough to buy things that cost more than you have to spend in one week or month. It's a way God helps you get ready for the future He's planned for you—like college, trade school, or university. Sometimes God uses your savings to prepare you for unexpected things: when they happen you already have the money to deal with them. Also, saving gets you ready to help people.

When you save wisely—for a special purpose such as college, to buy something you need or want (like a hamster), or to help someone—you're trusting God to look after your future. Saving just to have lots of money is foolish. It's trusting yourself not God. Instead, save wisely and trust God to care for you.

Little by Little

The secret to saving is bit by bit. No matter how young or old you are, you can start the habit of saving. Begin when you're young and you'll have the habit when you're older.

Start out small. Set yourself a "small goal" that will take you a few weeks to save for. Choose something you're excited about. Once you've met your goal and bought that thing you've longed for, you'll want to set another goal right away. You'll be hooked on saving!

Also set yourself a "big goal," one that will take longer than your small goal to save for. Don't set a huge one your first time. If your first big goal takes years, you'll probably get discouraged. Find one that will take a few months. As you get older, set bigger and bigger goals. Soon you'll be saving for college and a car!

Larry Burkett's Money Matters for Kids™ provides practical tips and tools children need to understand the biblical principles of stewardship. **Money Matters for Kids**™ is committed to the next generation and is grounded in God's Word and living His principles. Its goal is *"Teaching Kids to Manage God's Gifts."*

Money Matters for Kids™ and **Money Matters for Teens**™ materials are adapted by **Lightwave Publishing**™ from the works of best selling author on business and personal finances, **Larry Burkett.** Larry is the founder and president of **Christian Financial Concepts**™, author of more than 50 books, and hosts a radio program "Money Matters" aired on more than 1,100 outlets worldwide. Money Matters for Kids™ has an entertaining and educational Web site for children, teens, and college students, along with a special **Financial Parenting**™ Resource section for adults.

Visit Money Matters for Kids Web site at: **www.mm4kids.org**

building Christian faith in families

Lightwave Publishing is a recognized leader in developing quality resources that encourage, assist, and equip parents to build Christian faith in their families.

Lightwave Publishing also has a fun kids' Web site and an internet-based newsletter called *Tips & Tools for Spiritual Parenting.* This newsletter helps parents with issues such as answering their children's questions, helping make church more exciting, teaching children how to pray, and much more.

For more information, visit Lightwave's Web site: **www.lightwavepublishing.com**

MOODY
The Name You Can Trust
A MINISTRY OF MOODY BIBLE INSTITUTE

Moody Press, a ministry of Moody Bible Institute, is designed for education, evangelization, and edification.

If we may assist you in knowing more about Christ and the Christian life, please write us without obligation:

Moody Press, c/o MLM Chicago, Illinois 60610.
Or visit us at Moody's Web site: **www.moodypress.org**